D0547892

RW
ACC. No: 07058642

For Alice and Archie,
always my inspiration - S.H.

For Aimee and Alfie xx - H.S.

SIMON & SCHUSTER
First published in Great Britain in 2019 by Simon & Schuster UK Ltd
1st Floor, 222 Gray's Inn Road, London, WC1X 8HB • A CBS Company
Text copyright © 2019 Sam Hay • Illustrations copyright © 2019 Helen Shoesmith
The rights of Sam Hay & Helen Shoesmith to be identified as the author and illustrator
of this work has been asserted by them in accordance with the Copyright, Designs
and Patents Act, 1988 • All rights reserved, including the right of reproduction in
whole or in part in any form • A CIP catalogue record for this book is available from
the British Library upon request.
978-1-4711-8379-9 (PB) • 978-1-4711-8380-5 (eBook)
Printed in China • 10 9 8 7 6 5 4 3 2 1

A CAT'S CHRISTMAS CAROL

Sam Hay & Helen Shoesmith

SIMON & SCHUSTER
London   New York   Sydney   Toronto   New Delhi

It was closing time at the
Department Store on
Christmas Eve.

The cash tills
were quiet.

The doors were locked.
And the lights were turned down low.

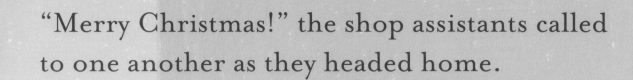

"Merry Christmas!" the shop assistants called
to one another as they headed home.

But someone wasn't at all excited about Christmas.
Clawdia, the security guard's cat!

"Bah! Christmas is for silly billies!" Clawdia grumbled, as she prowled the corridors on the lookout for mice.

She shivered. A window had been left open and a chilly breeze was blowing in.

But that wasn't the only thing coming in!

"STOP!"
Clawdia growled.

"But it's C-C-Christmas," the visitors squeaked. "And we're so c-c-cold."

"Rules are rules, even at Christmas," Clawdia said.

But the mice weren't giving up. "Run!" they squeaked.

Off they went . . .

Up, down,
round and round.

Past pots and pans

and globes and fans.

Round desks and chairs
and china bears, until —

"STOP!"

Clawdia was just about to pounce when the
mouse pointed to one of the televisions.

"Look!" it squeaked.
On the screen appeared a little lost kitten.

Clawdia suddenly had a memory of when she'd been lost,
looking for somewhere warm to sleep, just like the mice.

Clawdia was so busy thinking about the past,
she didn't notice the mouse escape.

But she was soon back on the hunt.

In! Out! Around! About!

Through shoes and frocks
and hats and clocks.

Past buttons and threads
and cushions and beds, until —

"STOP!"

Clawdia was just about to pounce
when the mouse pointed to the table.

"Isn't it lovely!" the mouse squeaked.
"Wouldn't it be perfect for a
Christmas party?"

Clawdia looked at the crackers and presents
and treats and sweets and shiny lights.

She imagined a family sitting there: the fun,
the laughter, the tasty titbits under the table . . .

Clawdia was so busy daydreaming,
she didn't notice the mouse escape.

But she was soon back on the hunt.

Ducking and diving,
dodging and driving!

Past diggers and rockets
    and pets-for-your-pocket.

Round dragons and knights,
    then snowmen and lights,
    and up until —

"STOP!"

Clawdia was just about to
pounce when the mouse
pointed down to the ground.

"Look!" it squeaked.
"What a strange cat.
I wonder what it's doing here?"

Clawdia gasped. Had the store replaced her with a robot . . . .

She imagined her future, thrown out into the snow; cold, unwanted and alone.

"Don't cry," squeaked the mice. "The store may not want you but we do! Why don't you spend Christmas with us?"

Clawdia wasn't sure. Mice were NOT allowed. And rules were rules, even at Christmas.

But maybe it didn't matter any more.
And Christmas with the mice did sound fun!

The mice found some yummy snacks and played lots of games.

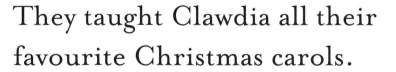

They taught Clawdia all their favourite Christmas carols.

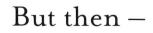

But then —

"Someone's coming,"
Clawdia whispered.
"Quick! Hide!"

This is it, she thought.
I'm about to be thrown
out into the snow.

"There you are, Clawdia," said the security guard.
"I see you've found your Christmas present — Kitty Bot!
It's going to do your job for you, so you can come home
with me for Christmas."

Clawdia couldn't believe her whiskers: a Christmas
present AND a family to celebrate with? For her?

Clawdia had the BEST time ever.

And so did the mice.

Because Christmas with friends was the best gift of all.